A KWANZAA MIRACLE

BY SHARON SHAVERS GAYLE
ILLUSTRATED BY FRANK NORFLEET

Troll

This book is dedicated to my family—
Parker, Amy, Toni, and Marvin—
and family celebrations everywhere!

—S.S.G.

To Trace and Artis

—F. N.

Ashley Parker and her brother, Darryl, thought December was the best month out of the whole year.

"It's a month of miracles," Ashley told Darryl one day while they were outside playing in the snow.

"Yep," agreed Darryl, scooping up a big mound of snow between his mittens. "First comes Christmas, then Kwanzaa starts the very next day."

Suddenly a big shadow loomed over Darryl and Ashley. It was Mrs. Jackson, the meanest lady in the whole building.

"Haven't I told you kids not to leave your toys all over the sidewalk?" she said sharply.

"Sorry, Mrs. Jackson," said Darryl and Ashley quietly. It seemed as though Mrs. Jackson was always scolding them.

"Ashley, Darryl!" called their mother, as she stuck her head out of their second-floor apartment window. "Our Kwanzaa planning meeting is about to start. Hurry up inside." Mrs. Parker looked down at Mrs. Jackson. "Hello, Rose!" she called. "Do you think you'll be able to join us this year?"

"Hrrummph," was Mrs. Jackson's only reply.

Ashley and Darryl hurried inside, happy to escape mean old Mrs. Jackson.

The children arrived at their apartment to find it filled with neighbors. Darryl and Ashley looked around the room. They recognized all the people who lived in their apartment building. Everyone was there—except Mrs. Jackson.

"Welcome to our annual Kwanzaa planning meeting," Mr. Parker called out, trying to get everyone's attention.

"Our first mission is to select a theme for this year's Kwanzaa celebration. I suggest we make Umoja, the first principle of Kwanzaa, the theme for our party. After all, Umoja means honoring our family, community, nation, and race—and that seems the right spirit for this celebration."

Then Mrs. Parker stood up. "Does anyone else have suggestions for ways we can honor Kwanzaa?"

Benisha Thompson, who lived on the third floor, raised her hand. Everybody in the building called her Benny. "I think our Kwanzaa celebration should have an honorary ancestor," she said.

Everyone loved Benny's idea. "But who should we choose?" asked Ashley.

For a few minutes there was silence, then Mrs. Parker said, "Let's all spend the next few days thinking about it. I'm sure we'll come up with the right person."

A few days later, Darryl and Ashley were outside having the most wonderful snowball fight. Darryl saved his very best snowball until the fight was almost over. He knew Ashley was good and tired, so he took aim and fired.

But instead of hitting Ashley, the snowball hit Mrs. Jackson's window!

The window instantly flew open.

"I want to see you kids in here right now!" called Mrs. Jackson. "I've got something to say to the two of you!"

Darryl and Ashley were really scared this time. They slowly climbed the front steps of their apartment building. In the front hallway, they shook off every flake of snow and carefully wiped their boots on the doormat. When they were sure they couldn't put it off any longer, they quietly knocked on Mrs. Jackson's door.

Darryl and Ashley expected the worse. They expected Mrs. Jackson to yell, or frown, or maybe even give them a scolding. Instead, she surprised the children by inviting them inside for some hot cocoa and oatmeal cookies.

"You aren't mad at us?" said Darryl, as they all settled on the couch.

"No," said Mrs. Jackson kindly. "You see, my little girl once broke a window during a snowball fight, too."

"You had a little girl?" Darryl and Ashley exclaimed in unison.

"Yes, but she died when she was just a child. Would you like to see her picture?"

"Yes!" said Ashley and Darryl together again.

As Mrs. Jackson showed Darryl and Ashley her family photo albums, she told them how much she missed her daughter and her husband, who had just recently passed away.

"You mean you don't have any family left?" asked Darryl.

Mrs. Jackson didn't say anything for a moment. "Just my sister," she said quietly, "but she lives all the way in Johnstown, so we don't get to see each other often."

Ashley and Darryl looked through the albums a little while longer. Then they thanked Mrs. Jackson for the cocoa and cookies. On the way up to their own apartment, they were very quiet.

At dinner they told their parents all about the snowball fight and their visit with Mrs. Jackson.

"You know, Mrs. Jackson's not so bad—" said Ashley.

"And," said Darryl, interrupting Ashley, "her oatmeal cookies taste just like Grandma's!"

At bedtime, Mr. and Mrs. Parker came in to kiss Ashley and Darryl good night.

"Daddy, Ashley and I were just thinking," said Darryl.

Mr. Parker chuckled. "Oh, and what were you thinking about?"

Ashley gave out a little squeal. "We think Mrs. Jackson should be our honorary ancestor for Kwanzaa!"

"What a wonderful idea!" exclaimed Mrs. Parker. "I'll call our neighbors tonight, then you two can ask her tomorrow morning, right after breakfast."

Mr. and Mrs. Parker kissed Ashley and Darryl one more time, turned out the lights, and went into the living room.

"You know, Mrs. Jackson once gave me her sister's phone number in case of an emergency," said Mr. Parker.

Mrs. Parker smiled. "I remember. And I was just thinking the same thing!"

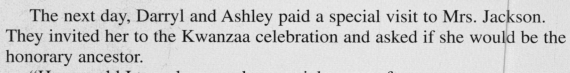

The next day, Darryl and Ashley paid a special visit to Mrs. Jackson. They invited her to the Kwanzaa celebration and asked if she would be the honorary ancestor.

"How could I turn down such a special request from my two new friends?" Mrs. Jackson asked, clapping her hands with delight. "I'd be honored to attend."

Darryl and Ashley hugged their neighbor before they ran home to tell their parents the good news.

During the following few weeks, the whole building prepared for Kwanzaa. Ashley and Darryl were especially busy helping their parents get ready for the festivities.

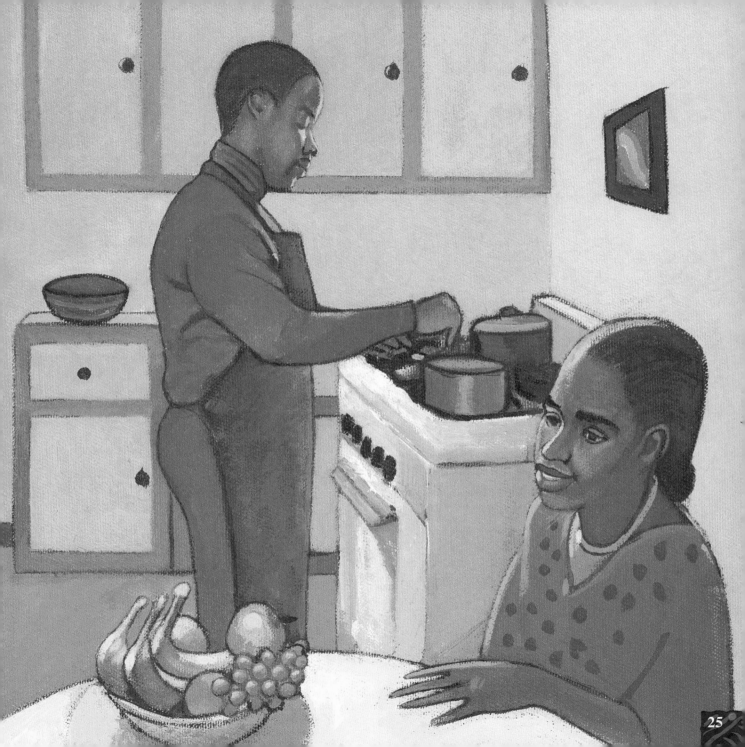

Finally the first day of Kwanzaa arrived. When it was time for the festivities to begin, Darryl escorted Mrs. Jackson to the party.

"Ssh!" Ashley whispered. "Here comes Mrs. Jackson."

When Darryl and Mrs. Jackson walked through the door, the old woman opened her mouth in surprise. "Sister!" she cried. Mrs. Jackson and her sister ran into each other's arms and hugged each other tight.

"Let's celebrate!" said Mr. Parker.

The Kwanzaa festivities were a big success. Everyone enjoyed the food, music, dancing, and company of friends and family.

Then it was time to honor Mrs. Jackson. When Mr. Parker gave the signal, Ashley ran up to Mrs. Jackson with a bouquet of flowers.

"Mrs. Delthea Jackson," Ashley called out loud and clear, "we name you our honorary ancestral grandmother."

Mrs. Jackson graciously took the flowers from Ashley. Then she stood up and faced the group. "Thank you all, especially Ashley and Darryl, for this wonderful honor. And thank you to my sister for coming to share this special time with me. You have all given me a Kwanzaa miracle!" Then she smiled the biggest, brightest smile they had ever seen.

"Happy Kwanzaa!" Darryl and Ashley shouted.

The Seven Principles of Kwanzaa

Nguzo Saba

1 Umoja (Unity)

To strive for and maintain unity in the family, community, nation, and race.

2 Kujichagulia (Self-determination)

To define ourselves, name ourselves, create for ourselves, and speak for ourselves instead of being defined, named, created for, and spoken for by others.

3 Ujima (Collective Work and Responsibility)

To build and maintain our community together, to make our sister's and brother's problems our problems, and to solve these problems together.

4 Ujamaa (Cooperative Economics)

To build and maintain our own stores, shops, and other businesses, and to profit from them together.

5 Nia (Purpose)

To make our collective vocation the building and developing of our community in order to restore our people to their traditional greatness.

6 Kuumba (Creativity)

To do always as much as we can, in the way we can, in order to leave our community more beautiful and beneficial than when we inherited it.

7 Imani (Faith)

To believe with all our heart in our people, our parents, our teachers, our leaders, and the righteousness and victory of our struggle.

—Dr. Maulana Karenga
September 7, 1965